Under the Lemon
MOON

BY *Edith Hope Fine*

ILLUSTRATED BY *René King Moreno*

Lee & Low Books Inc. • New York

abuela (ah-BWEH-lah): grandmother

abuelita (ah-bweh-LEE-tah): grandma

gracias (GRAH-see-ahs): thank you

hermosos (ehr-MOH-sohs): lovely (pl.)

la anciana (LAH ahn-see-AH-nah): the old one

limones (lee-MOH-nehs): lemons

lo siento (loh see-EHN-toh): I am sorry

mercado (mehr-KAH-doe): market

mi arbolito (MEE ahr-boh-LEE-toh): my little tree

m'ija (MEE-hah): my daughter

mira (MEE-rah): look

mira y recuerda (MEE-rah ee reh-KWER-dah): look and remember

qué grandes (keh GRAHN-dehs): how big (pl.)

qué jugosos (keh hoo-GOH-sohs): how juicy (pl.)

recuerda (reh-KWER-dah): remember

siembra las semillas (see-EHM-brah lahs seh-MEE-yahs): plant the seeds

Text copyright © 1999 by Edith Hope Fine
Illustrations copyright © 1999 by René King Moreno
All rights reserved. No part of the contents of this book may be reproduced
by any means without the written permission of the publisher.
LEE & LOW BOOKS Inc., 95 Madison Avenue, New York, NY 10016
leeandlow.com

Manufactured in China by RR Donnelley Limited, December 2015
Book Design by Christy Hale
Book Production by The Kids at Our House

The text is set in Weiss
The illustrations are rendered in watercolor and pastel

(HC) 15 14 13 12 11 10 9 8 7 6
(PB) 20 19 18 17 16 15 14
First Edition

Library of Congress Cataloging-in-Publication Data
Fine, Edith Hope
Under the lemon moon / by Edith Hope Fine; illustrated by René King Moreno. — 1st ed.
p. cm.
Summary: The theft of all the lemons from her lemon tree leads Rosalinda to an encounter
with la Anciana, the Old One, who walks the Mexican countryside helping things grow,
and an understanding of generosity and forgiveness.
ISBN 978-1-880000-69-4 (hardcover)   ISBN 978-1-58430-051-9 (paperback)
[1. Lemon—Fiction. 2. Generosity—Fiction. 3. Forgiveness—Fiction. 4. Mexico—Fiction.]
I. Moreno, René King, ill. II. Title.
PZ7.F495674Un 1999   [E]—dc21   98-45416
CIP AC

To Holly, a friend with a dream—E.H.F.

To my parents, Barry and Ruth Ann, with love—R.K.M.

Deep in the night, Rosalinda heard noises.

Wsss—Shhh—Snap!

What is that? she wondered, slipping from her bed. She peeked out past Mamá's garden with its Papá-clothes scarecrow and past the wash line.

Way back by the lemon tree, something was moving.

Heart thumping, Rosalinda crept to the doorway. Blanca, her pet hen, fluttered down from the rafters.

"Puc-buc-buc," brawked Blanca.

"Chhhht," shushed Rosalinda. The lemon wedge moon gave only a sliver of light. She waited for her eyes to grow used to the darkness.

Then she saw branches shaking in the shadows. Rosalinda looked harder. A man with hunched shoulders was stuffing lemons into a cloth sack. Her lemons. From her tree.

With Blanca under her arm, Rosalinda slipped out and hid behind the scarecrow.

Who is this Night Man? Why does he take my lemons? she wondered.

"Skr-a-a-a-wk!" Blanca flew to the scarecrow's head.
Rosalinda wobbled its stick-stiff arms.
"Ai-eee!" cried the Night Man. He grabbed the sack and fled.

In the morning, Rosalinda touched the stump of a broken branch. Not a single lemon was left on the whole tree.

A tear slid down her cheek.

"*¡Oh! Mi arbolito. Mi arbolito,* my little tree." Rosalinda crooned a sad song

as Blanca brawked along. She loved her lemon tree almost as much as she loved Blanca.

"Why, Blanca? Why did he do this?" Rosalinda asked, clutching a bundle of twigs.

Blanca's feathers drooped.

By the end of the week, many leaves of the lemon tree were yellow. Some had fallen. Rosalinda's worries got bigger—first the Night Man, now her tree was sick.

After breakfast, Rosalinda listened to the THRUM-THRUM of Mamá's loom. "I must do something," Rosalinda told her parents.

"Perhaps someone we know can help," Mamá suggested, smoothing Rosalinda's long hair.

"A neighbor or friend. Or your *abuela,*" added Papá with a hug. He turned back to his work bench.

Rosalinda set out.

    "My tree is sick. What should I do?" Rosalinda asked her neighbor,
Esmeralda.

    "I talk to my plants," said Esmeralda, tending her lush flower garden.
I did that, thought Rosalinda. Aloud she said, *"Gracias."*

She caught up with Señor Rodolfo, her friend of few words.

"My tree is sick. What should I do?" she asked.

"Much water," he said, heading for the nearby *mercado*, the market place.

I did that, thought Rosalinda. She remembered the heavy buckets of water she had lugged to her tree. Aloud she said, *"Gracias."*

When Rosalinda arrived at her grandmother's house, Abuela was sitting on her porch in the morning sun. Rosalinda settled in close to her, watching Abuela's knitting needles flash.

"What should I do for my tree, Abuela?"

"It will take time for your tree to heal, *m'ija*," she said. "I will light a candle for you."

I haven't done that, thought Rosalinda. Aloud she said, *"Gracias, Abuelita."*
Abuela eased the worries from Rosalinda's forehead with her warm hand.
"The candle will help, Rosalinda," Abuela said quietly. "Perhaps it will
summon La Anciana, the Old One. She helps things grow."

Everyone had heard rumors of La Anciana, of her powers for bringing
rain and making crops grow strong and tall. "Tell me again, Abuela," said
Rosalinda.

"For many years of full moons," Abuela began, "it has been said there
lives an old wise woman with gentle eyes. She walks the countryside
helping things grow."

"Where can I find her?" asked Rosalinda.

"No one knows, but they say La Anciana will come when she is needed."

Rosalinda thought hard: I need you. Please come, Anciana.

All day and night Rosalinda waited but La Anciana did not come.

"Be back by sundown," called Papá as Rosalinda and Blanca left the house early the next morning. Rosalinda waved.

She walked and walked, searching. Blanca puc-buc-buc'ed at her heels. Everywhere they went, Rosalinda called, "Anciana! Anciana!"

La Anciana did not answer.

"Maybe she isn't real," Rosalinda said to Blanca.

"Buh-brawk?" clucked the hen, as if she understood.

As the sun slipped down the sky, Rosalinda told Blanca, "We must go home." They circled back through the *mercado* with its colorful stalls and busy shoppers.

Then Rosalinda stopped. *Limones*, said a sign on the last stall. Behind a man, a woman rocked a baby. Their two small children played nearby with pebbles.

Rosalinda knew this man with hunched shoulders who was selling lemons.
He was the Night Man and the lemons were hers.

Rosalinda shivered. She and Blanca ducked behind a stall lined with bright
marionettes. "It's the Night Man! With lemons from my tree! Where . . .
where are you, Anciana?" stammered Rosalinda. She stroked her quivering
hen's soft feathers.

"I am here," came a low, sweet voice. Rosalinda jumped. Before her stood a woman with silvery hair. Her wrinkles were deep, her eyes gentle.

Rosalinda knew. Filled with wonder, she couldn't speak.

"You have looked far for me, Rosalinda," the woman said. "Tell me."

The woman listened as Rosalinda whispered her story.

"To take your lemons was wrong," La Anciana murmured. "Perhaps he had a need."

From her flowing sleeve, La Anciana pulled a strong branch with tiny buds.

"*Mira.* Watch," said La Anciana. "*Recuerda.* Remember. The moon will be full tonight."

Rosalinda listened with her heart and mind as La Anciana spoke of how to heal the lemon tree.

That night, Rosalinda crept outside under the lemon moon. She closed her eyes. *Mira y recuerda.* Watch and remember.

Rosalinda tore an old rag into strips. She held La Anciana's branch against the stump of the broken branch of her lemon tree. They fit as naturally as a fat lemon fit in Rosalinda's cupped hands.

Round and round she pulled the ribbons of cloth, binding the two branches until they held as one. Moonbeams poured over the sickly tree, making yellowed leaves look silver.

Tired, Rosalinda curled up under her tree and dozed.

She woke with a start when Blanca brawked. Rosalinda rubbed her eyes, astonished. Her tree glowed golden in the night, dripping with lemons as big and round as baby moons.

Arms wide, Rosalinda danced around the shimmering lemon tree.
Blanca followed, wings a-flutter.

The next morning Rosalinda told Blanca, "I know what to do." She piled fat yellow lemons into a wooden cart. Blanca perched on the lemon pyramid. Off they went together.

Friends and neighbors greeted her on the way. One by one,
Rosalinda gave away the amazing lemons.

"¡Qué *grandes!* How big. *Gracias,*" said Esmeralda.

"*¡Hermosos!*" said Señor Rodolfo. "Lovely."

"¡Qué *jugosos!* How juicy. *Gracias,*" said Abuela.

When Rosalinda had given away all but one of her lemons,
she headed for the last stall of the *mercado*.

Rosalinda stared at the Night Man and he stared back. Then
her warm hand touched his cold, rough hand and she gave him
her last fat lemon.

"Lo siento. I am sorry." The man lowered his eyes.

Rosalinda found her voice. "*Siembra las semillas.* Plant the seeds," she told him. "Do it tonight, while the moon is still full."

The man was quiet. He tilted his head toward his family with their worn clothes and hungry faces.

"For you and for them," said Rosalinda.

"I will do as you tell me," he said.

Rosalinda smiled. With a "puc-buc-buc," Blanca flip-flapped into the little cart for the ride back home. She settled in, content.

Rosalinda felt content, too. Except for one fat hen, Rosalinda's cart was empty, but her heart was as full as a lemon moon.